Knights & Castles

By Cassie Mayer

BRIGHT
connections media

A World Book Encyclopedia Company

Bright Connections Media
A World Book Encyclopedia Company
233 North Michigan Avenue
Chicago, Illinois 60601
U.S.A.

For information about other BCM publications,
visit our website at http://www.brightconnectionsmedia.com
or call 1-800-967-5325.

Knights & Castles
ISBN: 978-1-62267-007-9

Printed in China by Toppan Leefung Printing Ltd.,
Guangdong Province
1st printing July 2012

Picture Acknowledgments:

The publishers gratefully acknowledge the following sources for photography. All
illustrations and maps were prepared by WORLD BOOK unless otherwise noted.

Front Cover: Exactostock/SuperStock

Classic Image/Alamy Images 19, 30, 38; CW Images/Alamy Images 27;
INTERFOTO/Alamy Images 22, 29, 54; nobleIMAGES/Alamy Images 56; North
Wind Picture Archives/Alamy Images 13, 45; PRISMA ARCHIVO/Alamy Images
48; Sonia Halliday Photographs/Alamy Images 34, 50; The Photolibrary
Wales/Alamy Images 57; The Print Collector/Alamy Images 20; TPM
Photostock/Alamy Images 39; AP Photo 33; Art Resource 26, 29, 44, 46, 48, 51;
Bridgeman Art Library 4, 14, 16, 23, 24, 25, 31, 40, 46, 49; Gianni Dagli Orti,
Corbis 31; Dreamstime 10, 11, 34, 35, 52; Bridgeman Art Library/Getty Images
38, 55; Hulton Archive/Getty Images 7, 13, 24; Imagno/Getty Images 55; Oli
Scarff, Getty Images 28; Roger Viollet Collection/Getty Images 47; Time Life
Pictures/Getty Images 32; Victor R. Boswell Jr., National Geographic/Getty Images
53; Win Initiative, The Image Bank/Getty Images 28; Istockphoto 8, 21; North
Wind Pictures 15; Shutterstock 4, 6, 10, 12, 32, 36, 40, 41, 50, 54, 58, 59, 60,
61; SuperStock 22, 43; age fotostock/SuperStock 57; Bridgeman Art
Library/SuperStock 54; Fine Art Photographic Library/SuperStock 42; The Art
Archive/SuperStock 36

CONTENTS

As you read, you may come across words you don't know. You can find the definitions of many words from this book in the Words to Know section on page 62.

Introducing the Age of Knights and Castles

Long ago, before there were cars, planes, computers, or television sets, knights rode out from castles to do battle. This happened in the period that historians call the Middle Ages (A.D. 400's-1400's)—the centuries between ancient and modern times in western Europe.

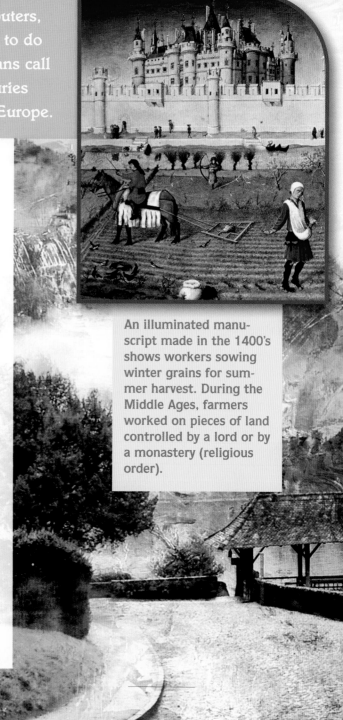

An illuminated manuscript made in the 1400's shows workers sowing winter grains for summer harvest. During the Middle Ages, farmers worked on pieces of land controlled by a lord or by a monastery (religious order).

What life was like then

In the Middle Ages, most people lived in small villages and rarely moved far from the place they were born. People in Europe knew little about Asia or Africa and nothing at all about America.

The great age of castle building in Europe lasted from about A.D. 1000 to 1500. Usually, a castle belonged to a king or to a landowner called a lord. The castle was built to keep out enemies, so it was a fortress as well as a home. Within its walls lived the lord and his best soldiers. These men wore a protective covering for the body called armor and rode into battle on horseback. They were called knights.

Europe during the 900's was poor, under-developed, and thinly populated. At least half the land could not be farmed because it was covered with thick forests or swamps. War, disease, famine, and a low birth rate kept the population small. People lived an average of only 30 years. There was little travel or communication, and less than 20 percent of the people went farther than 10 miles (16 kilometers) from their birthplace.

Did You Know?

The Middle Ages are also known as the *medieval period,* from the Latin words *medium* (middle) and *aevum* (age).

The end of an age

By 1500, the age of knights and castles was over. Gunpowder and cannon (tube-shaped guns too large to be carried by hand) could blast holes in the walls of the strongest castle. Armor was no protection against guns, either, so knights no longer rode into battle wearing heavy metal suits. Columbus had sailed from Europe to America, and a new age was beginning—the Age of Exploration.

People went on building castles, but now they were used as palaces and homes for wealthy people. Today, some castles are museums, full of treasures of the past. Tourists wander through rooms where knights once ate and slept.

IMPORTANT EVENTS OF THE AGE OF KNIGHTS AND CASTLES

A.D. 476	Fall of the Roman Empire in western Europe.
570?	Birth of the Prophet Muhammad, whose life and teachings form the basis of the religion of Islam.
400's-600	Angles, Saxons, and other peoples from Europe settled in England.
700	Maya civilization in Central America reached its peak.
732	Charles Martel, leader of the Franks, defeated Muslim invaders and halted the Muslim advance into Europe.
800	Charlemagne, king of the Franks, was crowned emperor of a new empire in western Europe.
790's-1100	Vikings from Scandinavia attacked England, Ireland, and other parts of western Europe.
1000	Viking explorer Leif Eriksson sailed from Greenland to North America.
1066	William the Conqueror led the Normans to invade England.
1096	First Christian Crusade to the Holy Land (Palestine). The last important Crusade ended in 1270.
1206	Genghis Khan became ruler of Mongolia. After conquering much of Asia, later Mongol rulers attacked eastern Europe in 1241.
1215	Magna Carta, or the Great Charter, was signed in England.
1271	Marco Polo left Italy to travel to China and did not return until 1295.
1337-1453	England and France fought the Hundred Years' War.
1300's-1600	The period known as the Renaissance, or "revival of learning," began, bringing new ideas in art and science.
1347-1352	A terrible disease known as the plague or Black Death swept across Europe.
1368-1644	The Ming dynasty ruled China after the end of Mongol rule.
1400's	The Aztecs built their empire in Mexico.
1455-1485	Civil wars known as the Wars of the Roses were fought in England.
1492	Columbus sailed to the New World.

Castles and Forts

Most of the castles still standing today are made of stone. Many such castles were built in Europe between A.D. 1000 and 1500. But long before then, people had built castles made of earth and wood.

Hilltop forts and towers

More than 3,000 years ago, people in Europe built forts on hilltops. A fort is a building or place that can be defended against an enemy. Forts are usually smaller than fortresses. Early European forts had walls made of turf or chalk dug out of the hillside. They were surrounded by earth banks and ditches for added protection. If an enemy attacked, the people took shelter inside the fort with their farm animals.

The Romans (citizens of the Roman Empire) made many forts in Europe. They built walls around towns and erected impressive defenses, such as Hadrian's Wall in northern England. Later, people in Scotland began to build broch—stone towers with no windows and only one door. Nobody actually lived in these towers, but people may have used them as shelter during attacks by raiders seeking slaves.

The Normans built the Tower of London after they invaded England in 1066. William the Conqueror, the first Norman king of England, needed the fortress to protect and control the capital city of London. The oldest part of the famous national monument is the great central tower, known as the White Tower. During the later centuries, the other parts of the fortress were built around the White Tower.

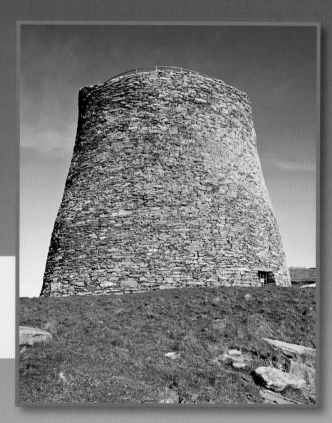

The Broch of Mousa in Shetland, Scotland, is one of the most well-preserved prehistoric buildings in Europe. Brochs date from about 500 B.C. to A.D. 200.

Fort-villages

About 500 B.C., Europeans began to build wooden forts with stockades—defensive walls that surrounded the fort. The gateways of these forts were protected by banks and ditches that served as barriers, making it hard for the enemy to storm the gate. The fort's defenders stood on top of the stockade, hurling spears and stones at the enemy. People felt safe inside the hill forts and built homes within their walls. In time, the forts became walled villages.

The Normans

The Normans were a group of Vikings. These raiders were originally from Scandinavia, a region of Europe that includes what are now Denmark, Norway, and Sweden. Between the 800's and 1000's, Norman warriors first seized northern France. From there, they went on to conquer England, southern Italy, and Sicily. They built stone castles as fortresses from which they could rule the lands they had won in battle. After conquering England in the late 1000's, they built one of their first castles, the White Tower, now part of the Tower of London. In the 1100's, the Normans invaded Ireland and built stone castles there, too.

The Normans contributed much to the English language and to English literature and architecture. At first, the Normans spoke French. Later, the Norman French blended with the language of the Anglo-Saxons (Germanic tribes that settled in what is now England in the A.D. 400's and 500's) and became English.

Why Is a Castle Called a Castle?

The word *castle* comes from the Latin word *castellum*. Latin was the language spoken by the ancient Romans, and a *castellum* was a small Roman fort.

Who Built the First Castles?

Huge stone fortresses were built in Greece and Turkey more than 3,000 years ago. Walled towns developed in the Middle East about 10,000 years ago.

Who Were First to Be Called Knights?

The word *knight* comes from the Old English word *cnight*, which means a household retainer. English people used the word to describe French mounted soldiers who first came to England after it was conquered in 1066 by Normans from the region of northern France called Normandy. These knights were warriors equipped and trained to fight on horseback.

The Bayeux (*bay YOO*) Tapestry tells the story of the Battle of Hastings, where the Normans defeated the English in 1066. The Bayeux Tapestry shows Norman knights on horseback charging the English, who are fighting on foot. The tapestry is more than 900 years old and is kept in a museum in France.

Parts of a Castle

A castle was a home, but not a very comfortable place to live. Castles were designed to make it difficult for anyone to capture them.

The strongest part of the first Norman castles was the keep, or central tower. However, some keeps were square, and if the enemy dug under one corner, the whole tower could fall down. For this reason, later castles had round or many-sided keeps.

Walls and towers

Most castles had an outer wall built around the top of a hill. Inside the wall was a central courtyard, called a bailey. Towers, connected by a walkway, were added at spaces along the wall. The towers had few entrances at ground level, so each one was a strong point for defense. If the wall was damaged in an attack, or if one tower was captured, soldiers in the other towers could continue fighting.

Dover Castle stands on a cliff near Dover, England, facing France across the English Channel. The keep of this famous castle was erected in the 1180's. The castle was built to defend the port against invaders.

Where Castles Were Built

- A good place to build a castle was on a hilltop. The castle guards could see enemy soldiers coming as they climbed the hill to attack the castle.
- Some castles were built inside cities as palaces and fortresses.
- Many castles were built to guard rivers and roads.

Gate and moat

The keep stood in the middle of the earliest castles, at some distance from the fiercest fighting. The first attack usually occurred at the main entrance to the castle, so a strong gatehouse was needed. Some later castles had the keep brought forward to serve as the gatehouse. The castle commander lived in the gatehouse and directed his soldiers in battle.

A ditch dug around the outer walls provided extra protection. Often this ditch, called a moat, was flooded with water. A narrow bridge called a drawbridge was the only way across the moat. The drawbridge could be raised when an enemy was sighted, so it kept invaders away from the castle walls.

Building castles

Builders chose the site of a new castle with care. They often used the same site on which earlier people had made a wooden fort. On flat land, the builders dug a ditch and piled up the soil to make a hill. Then they built their castle on top of the hill.

Did You Know?

When the Normans crossed the sea from France to invade England, they brought a wooden castle with them. The castle was made in sections that were quickly fitted together to make a fortress after the landing.

A typical castle had a moat filled with water crossed by a drawbridge. In this castle, the strongest point is the gatehouse, with its four towers. Other large towers defend the corners of the inner wall. ∨

The Knight's Castle

A castle belonged to a nobleman or lord who probably owned the land around the castle. Knights who fought for him also lived in the castle. They had to be ready to ride out on their horses and do battle at the lord's command.

Edinburgh Castle stands on Castle Rock, a huge rock overlooking the city of Edinburgh. Within the castle walls is the city's oldest building, the Chapel of St. Margaret, probably built in the 1000's.

Servants who cooked the lord's food and took care of his family also lived in the castle. From the safety of his castle, a lord could keep away his enemies—and control his own people. The same strong stone walls that could keep out an army could keep in a prisoner, so the castle was also a jail. A castle provided a fortress base from which the lord and his knights governed the surrounding region.

Alcazars

Spain has about 1,400 castles and palaces that were built in the Middle Ages. The Moors—Muslims from northwestern Africa who conquered part of Spain in the 700's, built many of the finest castles. (Muslims are believers in the religion of Islam.) The castles were beautifully decorated palace-fortresses called alcazars. *Alcazar* comes from the Arabic term *al-qasr*, meaning "the castle."

Even lords and nobles suffered difficult living conditions during the Middle Ages. Stone floors and walls, as seen in the keep (central tower) of Dover Castle, made for cold, harsh winters.

Life in a Castle

- The lord and his family lived in the castle.
- The lord entertained guests in the great hall.
- Religious services and prayers were held in the chapel.
- The lord slept on a bed. The servants slept on the floor with the dogs.
- Stone floors were usually covered with straw.
- Castles were gloomy. At night, people lit candles made of animal fat and torches made of wood.
- In winter, people kept warm around wood fires.
- Most windows had no glass. Only wooden shutters kept out the wind.
- Toilets often emptied into the moat.

Attacking a Castle

A siege was one way to attack a castle. During a siege, an army surrounded a castle for a period of time to try to force the people inside to surrender. A siege was a battle of wits and endurance between the attackers and the castle's defenders.

Attacking the walls

During a siege, attackers set up camp outside a castle. They tried to make holes in the castle walls by firing heavy stones from catapults (large slingshots for shooting stones and arrows) or from an early form of cannon. They dug tunnels under the castle walls to weaken them. They used battering rams (heavy wooden beams) to break down wooden gates. Some soldiers climbed ladders onto the wall. Others approached the castle inside wooden towers on wheels that were pushed up against the castle wall. Inside these siege towers, soldiers were protected from arrows and spears until they were close enough to fight the defenders on the castle wall.

Catapults were often used to attack castles and walled cities. The catapult worked like a giant slingshot to hurl heavy stones.

The First Tower, one of the most ancient fortifications in Italy, overlooks the city of San Marino. The fortification is surrounded by two sets of defensive walls.

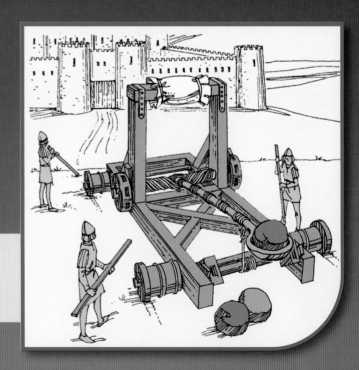

No surprise

When an army marched to attack a castle, the defenders usually had plenty of warning. First, riders galloped in with news of the enemy's approach, and soon the dust of marching soldiers and horses could be seen. Local people ran into the castle for shelter, bringing their pigs and cattle with them. Then they shut the castle's huge gates and pulled up the bridge across the moat with ropes or chains. Soldiers lined up behind the castle walls, ready to fight.

An army usually tried to capture a castle in two ways. First the soldiers tried to break through the walls. If that failed, they surrounded the castle and tried to force the defenders to surrender by preventing them from leaving the castle for food or other supplies. Eventually, the people inside the castle would run out of food and starve.

Soldiers used heavy wooden beams called battering rams to knock down the walls and open the gates of fortified towns and castles.

Defending the walls

Soldiers inside the castle fired arrows out of narrow slits in the walls and dropped stones onto the enemy. They often filled tubs with hot water or burning oil and poured it onto the attackers. They pushed away the enemy's ladders with long poles and tried to set fire to their wooden siege towers.

With plenty of food and water inside the castle, the defenders had a good chance of winning. The attackers often gave up and left after a week or so. But if the siege lasted months—or even years—the defenders eventually ran out of food or grew weak with sickness. Then they had to surrender and open the castle gates.

During a siege, attackers used such weapons as crossbows, cannon, and bows and arrows to break down a castle's defenses. ⬇

Life in the Middle Ages

By the 800's, most of the land in western Europe was split up into large estates ruled by rich lords. These estates were called manors. People on these lands lived in small villages. There were few towns or cities.

In the Middle Ages, most people were peasants (laborers of low social status) who lived by farming. They grew crops and raised animals to feed and clothe themselves. They also worked for the lord of the manor, on whom they depended.

Lord of the manor

The lord of the manor was usually a nobleman and a knight. His job was soldiering, and he took orders from his king. By pledging loyalty and promising to serve the king, the lord became the king's vassal. In return, the king granted him land. The granting of land in return for service was called feudalism. In western Europe, this system reached its height between the 800's and 1200's.

The lord controlled the land and collected taxes. He also judged disputes, kept an army of knights, and supervised the farming of his land.

A detail from an illuminated manuscript shows the elaborate clothing worn by the European upper class of the early 1400's. With the exception of men going to war, many nobles led a life of leisure.

Fiefs and vassals

Feudalism benefited knights and noblemen. For example, a nobleman, Sir John, pledged his loyalty to William the Conqueror, king of England from 1066 until his death in 1086. By promising loyalty, Sir John became the king's vassal. He promised to supply the king with 10 knights. In return, King William gave Sir John 20 manors to rule as his fief (piece of land). This meant that the land still belonged to the king, but it was entrusted to the lord— Sir John.

If the king called his army to battle, Sir John had to go. He also had to take nine other knights with him. Sir John might have to hire other knights to make up the number. As payment, he gave each knight a manor as a fief. The knight pledged his loyalty and service to Sir John. The knight was now Sir John's vassal.

Life on the Manor

The lord lived in a manor house or a castle. He had a garden, an orchard, farms and farm buildings, and peasants. Many manors also had a church, a mill for grinding flour, and a press for making wine from grapes and other fruits.

Peasants lived in huts clustered near the castle. A peasant farmed the lord's land, as well as any small plots of his own. He depended on the lord for protection from enemies and to give him justice in case of disagreements. Many peasants were serfs, which meant they were "bound to the land." Under the law, they were not free to move away. If a new lord took charge of the manor, the peasants remained with the land and had to work for the new lord.

Only wealthy nobles could afford elaborate meals—and the help of numerous servants. The life of nobles contrasted greatly with peasants, who lived in huts and subsisted on simple foods.

A peasant family worked together to farm the lord's land as well as their own.

In addition to farming his lord's land, a peasant also cut wood in the forest for the lord, stored his grain at harvest time, and repaired roads and bridges. Peasants had their own grain milled into flour at the lord's mill, baked their bread in the lord's oven, and took their grapes to the lord's wine press. Each time, they had to pay the lord. Peasants were usually paid in wheat, oats, eggs, or chickens.

Changing the crops

Fields on the manor were large and divided into strips. Each peasant worked several strips. They took care of plowing, sowing seeds, and harvesting the land. Each family farmed strips in different parts of the fields, so that good land and bad land were shared equally.

Farmers grew different crops in each field from one year to the next. This kept the soil fertile (able to produce crops) and helped prevent disease in plants. Farmers during the Middle Ages began to split farmland into three fields instead of two. They let one field lie fallow (empty) for a season so the soil would be fertile again for the next season. In the other two fields, they grew two different crops—perhaps wheat and beans. In this way, two-thirds of the land could be farmed each year instead of only half.

An illuminated manuscript from the 1500's shows peasants plowing fields and sowing seeds.

A simple home life

Peasants lived in bare huts. They slept on bags filled with straw and ate black bread (a heavy dark rye bread), eggs, and poultry. For vegetables, they grew beans, cabbages, and turnips. Meat was a special treat. Peasants were not allowed to hunt or fish because the wild animals, like everything else on the manor, belonged to the lord.

The Black Death

The Black Death was a deadly epidemic that spread across Asia and Europe beginning in the mid-1300's. By about 1400, the Black Death had killed up to 40 percent of the population of Europe—around 25 million people.

The Black Death transformed European society. It caused a labor shortage, and lords responded by enacting strict laws to try to keep peasants on their land and subject to traditional rents and other obligations. Some peasants rose up in bloody revolts. Others fled to the cities, where they could negotiate with landlords for better terms.

In the Middle Ages, people built their houses of stone or wood, often with thatched roofs (roofs made of dried grasses). Many houses had just one room. Others were long buildings with three or more rooms. Many small farm communities grew up near rivers, where people could use boats for travel and trade.

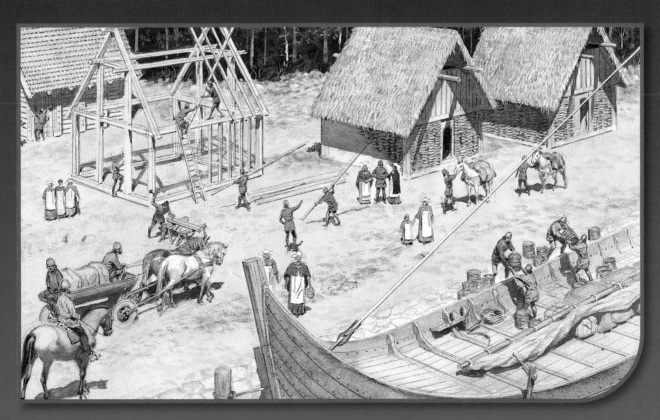

Becoming a Knight

A knight's training began when he was a boy. Instead of going to school, he learned how to behave correctly—and how to fight.

Once a man reached 21 years of age, he could become a knight in either one of two ways. The simplest way was on the battlefield, as a reward for bravery. Being tapped on the shoulder with a sword by another knight or a king made a man a knight.

In peacetime, a future knight had to undergo years of training. When he completed his training, he took part in a religious ceremony during which he pledged to use his weapons for sacred (holy) causes and ideals.

From page to knight

A boy training for knighthood left home when he was about 7 years old. First, he became a page, or student, in the household of a knight or a nobleman. There he learned to handle small weapons. He also learned the code of courtesy (polite behavior) expected of a knight.

At the age of 15 or 16, a page became a squire. He acted as a servant to his lord and rode with him into battle.

After about five years, a squire became a knight. For the religious ceremony, he took a bath, had his hair cut short, and prayed all night in church. In the morning, he received the sword and spurs of a knight.

A page learned to fight with swords. He also learned games of skill, such as chess, and hunted with trained hawks.

A squire waited on his lord. He tested his skill with a lance (long wooden spear) against a dummy target. In battle, he rode at his master's side.

The squire receives sword and spurs, becoming a knight.

The Age of Chivalry

The age of knights is often called the Age of Chivalry *(SHIHV uhl ree)*. *Chivalry* comes from the Old French word *chevalerie*, which means "horse soldiering." Over time, the term came to mean the code of behavior, or set of rules, by which a knight was expected to live. A knight who was guilty of cowardice or other serious misconduct was disgraced. His sword and his spurs were taken from him and broken.

In real life, a knight did not always live up to these high ideals. Sometimes his code of honor was applied only to members of his own high rank. Knights often acted brutally toward people of lower rank or toward those whose lands they conquered.

A True Knight Was Expected to:

- protect women and the weak
- champion good against injustice and evil
- love the land of his birth
- defend the church, even with his life

At tournaments, knights practiced their fighting skills. In this form of mock battle, each knight aimed a lance at the other.

Knights in Armor

When riding into battle, a knight wore a heavy suit of metal armor. Sometimes his horse was also armored. Many knights riding together made a colorful and impressive sight.

Chain mail

A knight wore armor to protect his body from arrows, swords, spears, clubs, and other weapons. The first knights wore a long piece of clothing, similar to a dress, made of padded cloth or leather. Over that, they put on a suit of chain mail, a kind of flexible armor made from tiny metal rings linked together. A Norman knight wore a chain-mail suit and a cone-shaped metal helmet. He carried a long spear, called a lance, and a shield that was large enough to protect most of his body.

A coat of chain mail was much too uncomfortable to wear all the time. The knight rolled it up and carried it on his horse. A man had to be strong to wear armor. A suit of chain mail weighed about 50 pounds (23 kilograms)!

English forces capture William I of Scotland (left) in the Battle of Alnwick of 1174. Knights in battle wore surcoats—gownlike pieces of clothing—over chain-mail armor.

Steel suits

Later, in the 1300's, helmets were stronger and covered the entire head. Knights also began wearing extra pieces of metal plate to cover parts of the body that chain mail did not protect well, such as the elbow, arm, knee, and leg. By the 1400's, knights wore complete suits of plate armor made of large pieces of steel. The suits had joints that allowed knights to walk and bend, but they were still clumsy.

Learning to wear armor

It was extremely hot and uncomfortable inside a suit of armor. A knight in training practiced putting on the armor in the correct order, or the pieces would not fit. He also practiced fighting in armor. He learned to ride his horse while wearing heavy armor and holding a lance and shield. And he learned to fight with a knight's weapons, such as a long sword and a spiked club.

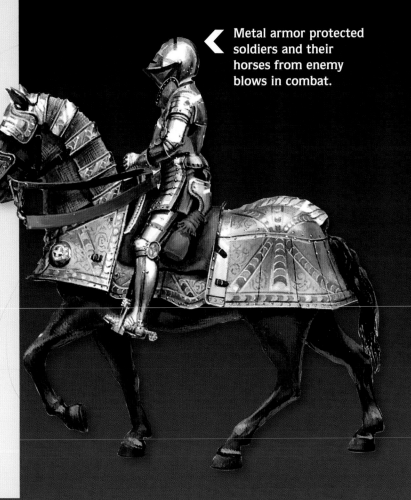

Metal armor protected soldiers and their horses from enemy blows in combat.

A Knight in Full Armor

Each piece of armor was made to fit the knight's body.

- A helmet protected the knight's head. The helmet had a visor that lifted up and down like a shutter.
- A collar made of chain mail protected the gap between the knight's helmet and the top of his body armor.
- The knight wore metal shoes and gloves called gauntlets.

Knights into Battle

When a knight rode into battle, he hoped his armor, weapons, and skill would bring him victory. Sometimes two knights faced each other in single combat, but most battles were fought between armies of knights and foot soldiers.

Choosing the ground

The battleground was often important in determining which side won. The Battle of Bannockburn in 1314 was one of the most important battles fought in Scotland. The Scots, led by Robert Bruce, saved their country from foreign rule by defeating the English. During the battle, the Scots fought from a better position than the English. The English knights were too crowded together to use their larger numbers skillfully and fled after suffering heavy losses.

In the Battle of the Lechfeld, fought in A.D. 955, Otto the Great—a German king who would be named the first Holy Roman emperor—drove Hungarian invaders out of the German states. Such battles were very chaotic. Knights were crowded together, fighting, falling to the ground, and being trampled under horses' hooves.

The battle-ax was a weapon used by knights in close combat.

In the June 1314 Battle of Bannockburn, the Scots managed to fight off the English, despite being outnumbered. It was a decisive battle in the First War of Scottish Independence. ➤

Down and out

Knights charging into battle on horseback were the armored tanks of their time. They usually smashed through enemy foot soldiers. But if a knight fell from his horse, he was in trouble. Plate armor was so heavy that he could not remount his horse without help, and he might not even be able to get to his feet. If the knight was lucky, he was captured. If not, he was killed by the enemy. Soldiers stripped dead knights of armor and weapons and took them as trophies.

Did You Know?

A king or an important lord captured in battle seldom was killed. He was worth more alive. He was held prisoner until his family or friends paid a sum of money called a ransom. In exchange for the ransom, the captive was freed. Some prisoners had to wait many years before the ransom money was paid.

Knights and Foot Soldiers

The army with the largest number of knights did not always win the battle. Some famous battles between knights and foot soldiers took place during the Hundred Years' War (1337-1453) between France and England.

A drawing made in the late 1400's shows English soldiers (above, right) fighting the French at the Battle of Crécy in 1346. In the actual battle (won by the English), bowmen would not have been so close to each other.

Knights against archers

The longbow ranked as the chief weapon of the English army when the Hundred Years' War began in 1337. The weapon was a large bow drawn by hand for shooting a long, feathered arrow. In 1346, in the Battle of Crécy *(KREHS ee)*, 7,000 English archers defeated a much larger French force that included more than 1,000 armor-clad knights.

The Battle of Agincourt

At the Battle of Agincourt *(AZH ihn koor)* in 1415, about 6,000 English soldiers with longbows defeated a French army of about 20,000 to 30,000. In this battle, the French knights became jammed together on muddy ground and had no room to swing their swords. Thousands of French knights were struck down by arrows, while others were trampled underfoot. English losses numbered in the hundreds, but there were at least 6,000 dead on the French side.

The crossbow was a powerful weapon. The archer used his foot to cock the bow string back for shooting.

Longbows vs. Crossbows

The English and Welsh were expert bowmen, or archers. Each archer carried a longbow as tall as himself! The bow was made of tough, springy wood, such as yew. The archer needed strong arms to bend his bow when he pulled back the bowstring. When he let go of the string, the bow shot a wooden arrow at great speed.

The longbow fired farther and faster than the crossbow, a weapon for shooting arrows that was also used during the Middle Ages. A crossbow could fire an arrow through a thick wooden door, but the crossbowman had to wind up his weapon with a handle each time he fired.

Spanish soldiers armed with pikes (spears with long wooden handles) enter the North African city of Tunis after its conquest in 1535. From the early 1200's to the late 1500's, Tunis was a center of trade between Africa and Europe.

The Knight and His Arms

Every knight had his own coat of arms—an emblem made up of pictures, colors, and symbols. Coats of arms were first displayed on the knight's shield. Later, they were shown on flags, clothes, and other personal possessions.

A knight's coat of arms was his "badge." It enabled his friends and followers to recognize him on the battlefield. Only knights had coats of arms, which were passed on to a son and heir. No two people could have the same coat of arms. A knight's coat of arms decorated his armor, horse covering, and shield.

Who's who?

When knights were covered in armor from head to foot, only an expert could identify them by their coats of arms. The people who knew about coats of arms were called heralds. Heralds were first used to carry messages between kings or armies, and they had to know whether a knight was a friend or an enemy.

Heralds were later given the job of deciding which new design could be allowed for a coat of arms. They made sure that no two people had the same coat of arms and that no one falsely claimed to be a member of a noble family.

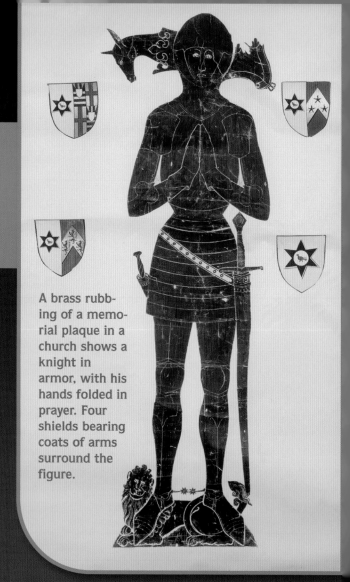

A brass rubbing of a memorial plaque in a church shows a knight in armor, with his hands folded in prayer. Four shields bearing coats of arms surround the figure.

Shields were decorated with various colors, designs, and lines that became standard. Each style had a name.

Legend of the Unicorn

Most coats of arms include an object or figure, such as a unicorn. The unicorn was a legendary animal, with the head and body of a horse, the legs of a deer, and the tail of a lion. It had a single horn in the middle of its forehead.

It was once believed that the unicorn's horn protected people against poison. Powders said to be made of unicorn horn were sold for very high prices. Most scholars believe that the image of the unicorn was based on muddled reports of the rhinoceros.

Buried under brass

When a knight died, his grave was often covered by a decorative brass plate. About 10,000 of these "brasses" are left in England. The oldest surviving brass in England was made in memory of Sir John d'Aubernoun, a knight who died in 1277. It can be seen in Stoke D'Abernon, a small village in Surrey.

Most brasses date from between 1350 and 1650. They show knights in armor, sometimes pictured with their wives, and tell us much about the clothing of the time. Brasses are often set into the floors of old churches, and many cover graves.

Rubbing over the brass with wax on paper produces a copy, a "rubbing," of the picture. However, the practice is now discouraged because the friction from rubbing wears away at the brass.

Brasses that cover graves are metal plates. They are usually engraved with a picture of the person they honor.

Knights served the king, who was the supreme ruler. A noble lord might have many manors and many knights, but he was still the king's servant. During the Middle Ages, most people believed that a king was God's chosen ruler on Earth, so it was wrong for anyone to disobey a king.

Crowning a king

A king or a queen wore a crown as a symbol of supreme authority. Knights were present at a king's coronation (crowning ceremony). In Christian kingdoms, coronations took place in a church or cathedral and included a religious service.

From the time of William the Conqueror, who became king in 1066, English kings and queens have been crowned in Westminster Abbey in London. During the ceremony, the new monarch sits in the Coronation Chair. Beneath the chair is the Stone of Scone. On this stone, Scottish kings sat to be crowned until King Edward I of England took the stone to England in 1296.

In 1996, Queen Elizabeth II had the stone moved to Scotland, where it is kept at Edinburgh Castle. The stone is to be returned to London temporarily whenever a monarch of the United Kingdom is crowned.

The Coronation Chair, used in the coronation of all British kings or queens, is 700 years old. The wooden chair was built to hold the Stone of Scone, which is now kept at Edinburgh Castle in Scotland, except for coronations. >

Kings and queens have been crowned in Westminster Abbey in London since 1066. The current Gothic structure was begun by Henry III in 1245.

The king's champion

After a new king was crowned, he and his guests sat down to a splendid feast. A fully armed knight then rode into the banquet hall. He was the king's champion and challenged to a fight any person who questioned the right of the new king to rule.

Paying homage

Every knight had to pay homage (respect) to the king to become the king's vassal. The knight knelt before the king and placed his hands between the king's, declaring that he was the king's follower. The king then raised the knight to his feet and kissed him. The knight often swore an oath upon the Bible or upon some holy object to show that he meant to keep his promise.

Crowned Heads

Crowns were worn by rulers in ancient Egypt and Assyria, a country that covered the northern part of present-day Iraq. The Greeks gave a crown of laurel leaves to their athletes as a symbol of victory. Roman emperors adopted this idea, but their crown of leaves were made of metal—usually gold. Rulers in Europe probably followed the Roman custom.

William I, the Conqueror, was crowned king of England on Christmas Day, 1066. William had won the crown by conquest when his Norman army defeated the English army and killed the English king, Harold.

Edward III, who ruled England from 1327 to 1377, pays homage to King Philip VI of France. Edward did not much like paying homage to Philip, but was forced to because his holdings in France made him something of a vassal to Philip.

The King and the Law

In England, the king was the head of government. His word was generally law, though he listened to the advice of lords and churchmen meeting in council. Even so, the king was not all-powerful. He was bound by his people's common laws. From these roots grew the idea of a responsible monarchy—a form of government in which one person is head of state for life.

Law and justice

In ancient times, customs and laws often differed from district to district. In England, where the laws were based on the customs of the people, similar cases were often judged differently in different districts.

In the early 1100's, strong English kings began to set up a countrywide system of king's courts. Judges moved around the country to hear cases, and they applied the same rulings in all similar cases. The courts set up rules known as common law that were applied equally everywhere in the country.

A picture from about 1450 shows a court of law known as the King's Bench. Prisoners in chains (bottom of image) wait to come before the judges (top). Around the table, clerks with long rolls of documents record the proceedings.

Crime and punishment

Laws were strict in the Middle Ages. Anyone found guilty of a serious crime, such as murder, forgery, robbery, or treason (disloyalty to one's ruler) could be sentenced to death. Punishment for stealing a neighbor's chicken might be payment of a fine, branding (burning a mark on the skin with a red-hot iron), whipping, or death. And anyone found killing deer in the king's hunting park faced almost certain death.

Dishonest shopkeepers who broke trading rules—perhaps by adding water to beer or selling underweight loaves of bread—were dragged through the streets and locked up in the town stocks, an old device used for punishment consisting of a wooden frame with holes for the limbs of the victim. Townsfolk came to jeer and throw rotten vegetables at them.

Women's rights

An unmarried woman had most of the same rights as a man, but a married woman could not own property without her husband's consent. Nor could a married woman be accused of a crime. A woman's husband was held responsible for any crimes she committed.

An image from a 1514 illuminated manuscript shows King Charlemagne *(SHAHR luh MAYN)* presiding over his royal court. Charlemagne, king of the Franks (parts of present-day France), conquered much of western Europe and united it under a great empire.

Did You Know?

Until about 1300, a person accused of a crime might be tried by ordeal. The accused person had to undergo a test, such as picking up a red-hot iron bar with a bare hand or picking a stone out of a pan of boiling water. If his burns healed within three days, it was declared that God had shown the person was innocent.

An image from an 1130 illuminated manuscript shows King Henry I of England having nightmares about the problems of being a king. Peasant farmers present a petition of complaints and requests, and angry lords threaten him with swords. Henry ruled England from 1100 to 1135.

Nobles Rebel

Despite their oaths of loyalty, lords sometimes rebelled against their king.

English lords present King John with Magna Carta in 1215. The act, which he was forced to sign, bound the king to rule within the law of the land.

King John

John of England was the youngest son of King Henry II. When John became king of England in 1199, he demanded more military service from the lords and sold royal positions to the highest bidder. He also raised taxes without the agreement of his barons (nobles).

The angry barons joined with the leaders of the church to demand that John meet them and agree to a list of their rights. After the barons raised an army to back up their demands, King John met them at Runnymede, a meadow near the River Thames southwest of London.

Magna Carta

The barons forced the king to sign an agreement known as Magna Carta, which is Latin for "Great Charter," or document. By signing it, the king promised to uphold the old established laws of the land.

Most of the charter benefited the barons. Parts of it granted the church freedom from the king's interference, and a few articles guaranteed the rights of the rising middle classes, such as town merchants. But ordinary people were hardly mentioned.

Magna Carta did not end the struggle between King John and the barons. A war broke out, and John died during the fighting. Later, Magna Carta came to be recognized as part of the basic law of England and of other English-speaking nations.

Parliament grows

King John's son, Henry III, also had trouble with the barons. A baron named Simon de Montfort led a rebellion against Henry. De Montfort summoned ordinary English citizens representing the local communities to discuss government matters with the barons and church leaders. This led to the growth of Parliament—a lawmaking body that represents all the people. Simon de Montfort's revolt ended when he was killed in battle in 1265, but the king was never again to rule unchallenged.

Why Magna Carta Was Important

Magna Carta ruled that the king must ask his barons for their advice and agreement in all matters important to the kingdom. Later, some parts of Magna Carta were used to declare that no law could be made without the consent of Parliament. Other parts of Magna Carta became the foundation for modern justice in many countries. One article in Magna Carta says that no free man shall be imprisoned, deprived of property, sent out of the country, or destroyed except by the lawful judgment of his peers (equals) or by the law of the land.

A canon (priest) at Salisbury Cathedral in England examines the best preserved of the four remaining copies of Magna Carta signed by King John in 1215.

The Church

The Christian Church was a unifying force in western Europe during the Middle Ages. The church touched almost everyone's life in many important ways.

Education

Church leaders took over many functions of government after the Roman Empire collapsed in the 400's. Two church institutions, the cathedral and the monastery, became centers of learning. Cathedrals were the churches of bishops—high-ranking officials in charge of an area containing a number of churches. Monasteries were communities of men who gave up worldly life to serve God through prayer and work.

The monks living at the monasteries, as well as the nuns and the churchmen at the cathedrals, helped continue the reading and writing of Latin, the principal language of western Europe for hundreds of years. They preserved many ancient manuscripts and founded most schools in Europe.

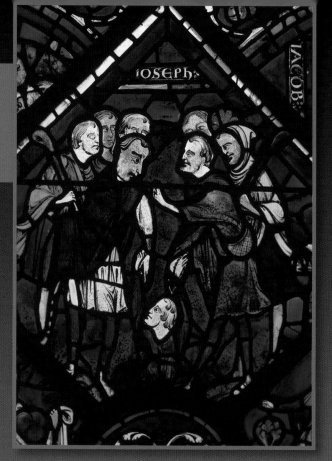

Detail of a window in the Chartres Cathedral in France (1200's). Stained-glass windows in churches often illustrated stories from the Bible in sparkling light and glowing colors. Few people in the Middle Ages could read, so the scenes helped teach Bible stories.

Gothic church architecture, such as the majestic Sainte Chapelle ("Holy Chapel") in Paris, was known for the soaring heights of interior spaces and enormous expanses of stained glass windows. Such tall, thin walls were made possible by exterior buttresses, stone structures that supported the walls from the outside.

Cathedral building

The greatest era of cathedral building occurred in Europe from around 1000 to 1500. Princes and laborers alike contributed money to build magnificent stone cathedrals that rose above medieval towns. Stained glass windows and sculptured figures that decorated the cathedrals portrayed events in the life of Christ and stories from the Bible. These scenes made up a visual encyclopedia of medieval knowledge for the many worshipers who could not read.

The power of the church

The church became the single great force that bound Europe together during the feudal period. The church baptized a person at birth, performed the ceremony at the person's marriage, and conducted burial services when the person died.

One great power of the church was its threat of excommunication. To excommunicate a person meant to cut the person off completely from the church and take away the person's hope of going to heaven. If a lord continued to rebel after being excommunicated, the church closed all the churches on the lord's land. No one on the land could be married or buried with the church's blessing. The people usually became so discontented that they rebelled, and the lord finally yielded to the church.

A divided church

The power of kings grew in the late Middle Ages, and bitter disputes arose between kings and church leaders. The pope and other church leaders took an increasing part in political affairs, and kings interfered in church affairs more often. There were also disputes within the church over the election of the pope—the head of the church. These disagreements weakened the power of the church.

The Romanesque-style Église St-Etienne in Caen, France, was completed in 1063 and predates the Gothic period of church architecture. Building such a structure was a huge undertaking that sometimes took decades, even centuries to complete.

Knights on Crusade

The Crusades were religious wars declared by the pope against Muslims in Palestine, sometimes called the Holy Land. They were organized mainly to defend Christians and to recover or defend territories that Christians believed belonged to them by right. Knights from all over Europe fought in these holy wars, which took place from the late 1000's through much of the 1200's.

A crusader castle—the Krak des Chevaliers—still stands in Syria. It was built in the 1100's by the Knights Hospitallers, a famous order of knights. The castle was big enough to house several thousand knights and withstood many Muslim attacks.

Aim of the Crusades

The original goal of the Crusades was to gain and keep control of Palestine, an area of land that lay along the eastern coast of the Mediterranean Sea. This region was important to Christians because it was where Jesus Christ had lived. Christian pilgrims from Europe journeyed to the city of Jerusalem and other holy places in Palestine.

In the 600's, Arab Muslims gained control of Jerusalem, but they still let Christians visit the city. Then, during the 1000's, Turkish peoples called Seljuks (*sehl JOOKS*) conquered Palestine. They were Muslims, too. But unlike the Arabs, they made it difficult for Christians to visit the holy places.

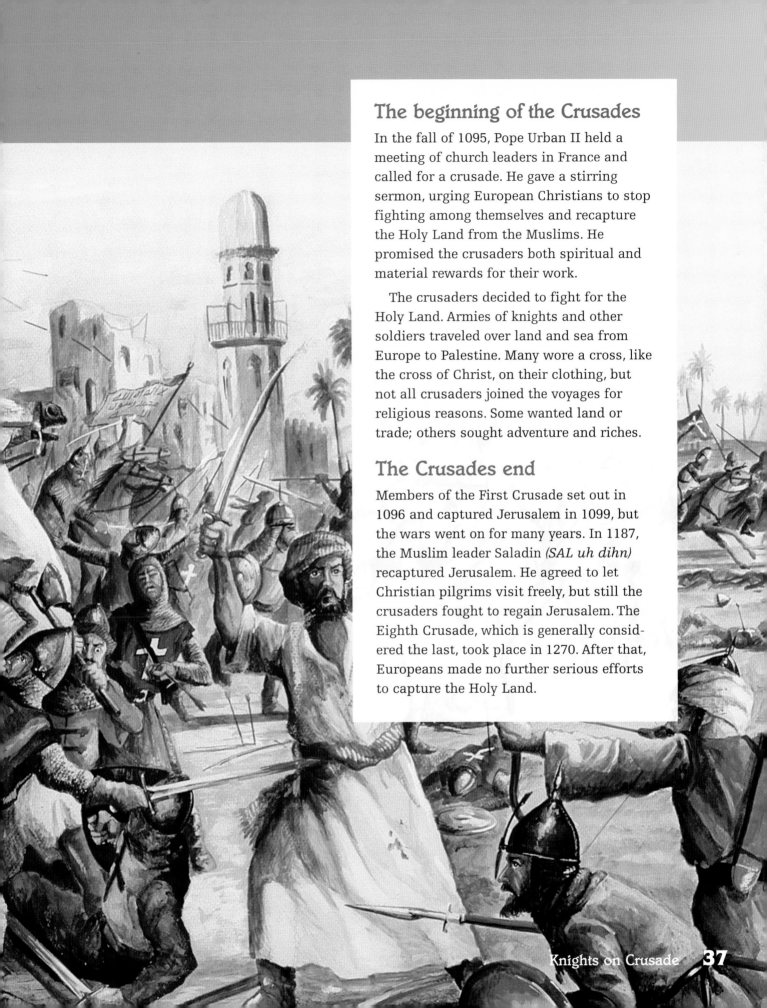

The beginning of the Crusades

In the fall of 1095, Pope Urban II held a meeting of church leaders in France and called for a crusade. He gave a stirring sermon, urging European Christians to stop fighting among themselves and recapture the Holy Land from the Muslims. He promised the crusaders both spiritual and material rewards for their work.

The crusaders decided to fight for the Holy Land. Armies of knights and other soldiers traveled over land and sea from Europe to Palestine. Many wore a cross, like the cross of Christ, on their clothing, but not all crusaders joined the voyages for religious reasons. Some wanted land or trade; others sought adventure and riches.

The Crusades end

Members of the First Crusade set out in 1096 and captured Jerusalem in 1099, but the wars went on for many years. In 1187, the Muslim leader Saladin *(SAL uh dihn)* recaptured Jerusalem. He agreed to let Christian pilgrims visit freely, but still the crusaders fought to regain Jerusalem. The Eighth Crusade, which is generally considered the last, took place in 1270. After that, Europeans made no further serious efforts to capture the Holy Land.

Learning and Knowledge

In the Middle Ages, many scholars and teachers were monks or priests. Few ordinary people even went to school, and most people could not read or write.

Book-making

Before the invention of the printing press in the mid-1400's, books were expensive treasures that had to be made by hand. This task fell to monks, who labored for years copying each book by hand. One group of monks made the parchment pages (writing material made of animal skins), and another group of monks wrote the letters. A third group of monks did the illumination. These colored decorations included animals, human figures, branches with leaves, geometric designs, and ornamental letters. A fourth group of monks bound the finished pages into books.

Most books made in western Europe were written in Latin, which had been the language of the Romans and was understood by educated people throughout Europe. It was also the language used in church. But by the 1300's, European authors began writing books in their own languages. Dante Alighieri *(DAHN tay ah leeg YEH ree)* wrote a long religious poem called *The Divine Comedy* in Italian. In England, Geoffrey Chaucer wrote *The Canterbury Tales* in English. This opened a new literary age and gradually helped to bring learning and literature to the common people.

Monks copied books by hand and decorated the pages. Each copy of a book took many hours to make.

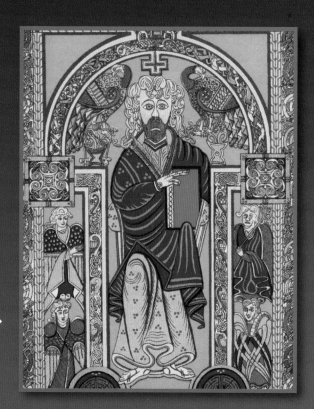

The Book of Kells is an illuminated manuscript that was produced between the mid-700's and early 800's, probably in a monastery in Ireland. It is considered one of the world's most beautiful books.

Universities

European universities developed from the cathedral and monastery schools. Their development took place so slowly that it is difficult to know the point at which they became universities. Many scholars believe the oldest European university is the University of Bologna in Italy. It came into existence about 1100. The University of Paris also developed in the 1100's. It became a model for other universities, including Oxford and Cambridge in England. Many other universities appeared in Europe in the 1200's and the 1300's.

These first schools were founded largely to serve the professions. They provided the first unified teaching of law, medicine, and theology (the study of religion).

Muslim scholars and learning

Over the centuries, western European scholars had studied and preserved many ancient Greek and Roman writings, but some works were lost. Meanwhile, some of those lost works had been preserved by Greek and, later, Muslim scholars. These works and many new ideas were brought to western Europe in the 1100's and 1200's by Muslim scholars from North Africa and Spain.

Muslim scholars brought another important change, too. They introduced people in Europe to the Hindu-Arabic numeral system, which we still use today. Prior to this, the universities had used the Roman numeral system, in which letters stood for numbers. The Hindu-Arabic numeral system made it easier to do calculations, especially in business.

Professors meet at the University of Paris sometime after it was founded in the 1100's. Universities developed gradually from groups of separate schools.

Did You Know?

The old Latin writing of Roman times used only capital letters and ran all the words together. In the Middle Ages, scribes developed a system of writing that was easier to read than Roman writing. They used capital letters and small letters, set up a system of punctuation, and left spaces between words.

The Arts

During the Middle Ages, the arts were mainly devoted to glorifying God and strengthening the power of the church. Artists worked for the church or for royal and noble families.

Medieval paintings were either small or very large. The small paintings included illuminated (decorated) manuscripts along with images of Christ and the saints. Most large paintings were murals, which were made on walls. Painters also designed tapestries and mosaics that decorated walls. Mosaics are made of many small pieces of stone, glass, or wood of different colors that form a picture or design.

The church's influence

Church leaders were conservative in their taste in painting. Artists were required to make good reworkings of earlier art, not create something new.

Artists who painted religious scenes made no attempt to show the world as it really was. The different sizes of the figures established an order in which Christ, the most important figure, is the largest. Artists used special colors or styles as symbols. For example, a sky painted gold or purple symbolized God's kingdom in heaven.

The Annunciation to the Shepherds by the French artist Simon Marmion (1425-1489) depicts an angel revealing to shepherds that a Savior, Christ the Lord, is born. In the Middle Ages, artists were mainly commissioned to create religious scenes.

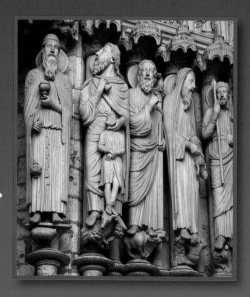

The entrance porches to Gothic Chartres Cathedral in France are enriched with statues of the apostles, saints, and other religious figures. Chartres was built between 1193 and 1250.

Romanesque

Romanesque painting and architecture flourished in Western Europe beginning about 1050. The typical Romanesque church had thick walls; thick, closely spaced columns; heavy arches; and small windows.

During this period, wealthy monasteries became the most important patrons of the arts. Many churches were built, and old buildings were enlarged and redecorated, often with large murals.

Gothic

Gothic is the name given to the art of the later Middle Ages, especially from the mid-1100's to about 1400. The Gothic style is associated with the age of cathedral construction in northern Europe. The style often is identified with such constructional devices as pointed arches, ribbed vaults, and flying buttresses.

Gothic architecture was noted for its immense size and height. Use of the flying buttress, introduced about 1175, reduced the amount of solid wall space needed for support, allowing the walls to be opened with large stained glass windows.

The interior of Amiens (*AM ee uhnz*) Cathedral in France—with its high columns, arched vaults, and light filtered through stained glass—is like a heavenly forest with light filtered through the leaves of towering trees. Construction of the Gothic cathedral began in 1220.

The builders of Gothic cathedrals channeled water off roofs with waterspouts carved into grotesque figures called gargoyles. Gargoyles were believed to ward off evil spirits.

People have always enjoyed listening to and telling stories. During the Middle Ages, few people owned books or could read or write. Many legends and stories were handed down by word of mouth.

Storytellers

Stories were told around the fire in the Great Hall of the castle and by the villagers in their homes. Wandering minstrels (professional entertainers) came to entertain the lord in his castle with stories of adventure and daring deeds. Singers called troubadours *(TROO buh dawrs)* composed love songs for noblemen and ladies. They told tales of noble kings, brave knights, and fair ladies. Some real-life knights made up stories of their own and exaggerated their real adventures.

King Arthur

King Arthur was a legendary ruler of England. Stories of King Arthur told how he led a band of Christian knights, including Lancelot *(LAN suh lot)* and Galahad *(GAL uh had)*. In their many adventures, they faced great dangers while searching for the Holy Grail. According to some versions of the legend, the Holy Grail was the cup used by Jesus Christ at the Last Supper before he was crucified (put to death by nailing the hands and feet to a cross).

A real Arthur probably existed, but historians know little about him. Storytellers may have based the tales on an actual British leader who won minor victories over German invaders in the early A.D. 500's. A Welshman named Geoffrey of Monmouth wrote the stories down about 1136, and they were then told and retold by other writers across western Europe.

An illustration from *King Arthur's Wood*, a medieval romance written and illustrated by the English artist Elizabeth Adela Stanhope Forbes. For almost 1,000 years, writers have told of Arthur's brave deeds and the adventures of his knights of the Round Table.

Robin Hood

Robin Hood was a legendary English outlaw who stole from the rich and gave to the poor. Many stories told of his daring, and he became a folk hero. According to the stories, Robin Hood and his followers lived in Sherwood Forest, near Nottingham, in the 1100's. Among Robin's companions were Friar Tuck, a fat, jolly monk; Little John, a giant of a man; and Maid Marian, Robin's sweetheart. In their adventures, the outlaws outwit their enemies.

No one knows whether the character of Robin Hood was based on a real person. According to one scholar, Robin Hood was actually the Earl of Huntingdon, and his real name was Robert Fitzooth. However, many other scholars believe that Robin Hood is a fictitious character.

Robin Hood and his outlaws were famous for their skill with bows and arrows. Their green clothing helped them hide among the trees of Sherwood Forest, where they lived. Robin Hood was seen as a hero of the common people against the unjust King John.

William Tell

William Tell was a legendary hero of Switzerland. He represented the spirit of the Swiss as they struggled for independence from Austrian rule in the 1300's. According to legend, the Austrian governor of Tell's canton (state) set a hat on a pole in the town square and ordered all Swiss to bow to it. When William Tell refused, he was arrested. The governor promised to free him if he could shoot an arrow off his own son's head. Tell, famous for his skill with a crossbow, did exactly that. But the promise was not kept and Tell remained a prisoner. He eventually escaped, killed the governor, and led a revolt against the Austrians.

The Canterbury Tales

The Canterbury Tales are stories written in verse by Geoffrey Chaucer, who lived from about 1340 to 1400. Chaucer was the greatest English poet of the Middle Ages. He was a learned man who traveled in Europe to manage relations between England and other countries. He also wrote for people at the court of the king. In *The Canterbury Tales*, he tells of a group of pilgrims traveling from London to the shrine of Saint Thomas Becket at Canterbury. On their journey, each pilgrim tells a tale to entertain the others.

In the Great Hall of the castle, the lord and his knights ate, drank, and played gambling games, such as dice. Outdoors, they entertained themselves by training for war. Knights fought mock battles and hunted wild animals.

An illustration from an illuminated manuscript from the 1400's shows nobles chasing a deer with hounds. Deer meat, or venison, was often served in noble households. The poor were not allowed to hunt or trap game.

War games

A knight spent much of his time exercising and training. He had to keep his body fit and strong to use heavy weapons, such as the sword and mace (a kind of club). Knights sometimes took part in jousts. In these contests, two knights—on horseback and in full armor—charged at each other. Each man tried to hit the other with his lance and knock him to the ground. The lances were usually fitted with blunt tips to prevent serious injury, but some knights fought to the death.

Groups of knights took part in other mock battles, which sometimes became so lifelike that men were seriously wounded or killed. Crowds of people gathered to watch these fights, as well as the archery contests and wrestling bouts that took place at the same time.

Hunting

Lords and ladies enjoyed hunting. They rode into the forests with packs of hunting dogs to chase deer, wild boar, and other animals. Kings often set aside huge areas of land for their own private hunting parks. Hawking was another popular sport. Hawks were trained to catch hares and such birds as pigeons or ducks.

Miracles and Farces

Some dramas of the Middle Ages were called miracle plays and morality plays. Miracle plays told stories from the lives of the saints or the Virgin Mary. Morality plays used a story to teach a moral lesson.

In time, professional actors began to perform plays. Some actors became part of noble households. They entertained guests with folk tales and comic skits between courses at banquets. These entertainments were called farces and interludes.

Ladies at home

The lord's wife was expected to sew, spin, weave, and to supervise the household servants, but her main responsibility was to give birth to male children. If she did not have at least one son, her husband could end the marriage. Some noblewomen took part in outdoor pursuits, such as hunting. Others passed their time making tapestry pictures woven from colored threads.

Watching a play

In the early Middle Ages, religious plays were performed in church. From the 1200's, plays were moved outdoors. The dramas of this time are often called "mystery" plays. Performances of these plays were then taken over by townspeople who were members of guilds, such as bakers, weavers, and silversmiths. They paid for the productions and acted in the plays.

In England, the setting for each play was mounted on a cart called a pageant wagon. The wagon was drawn through the city and stopped at various places, where the audience gathered to enjoy the performance.

Musicians, a juggler, and a jester entertain at a royal court during the Middle Ages. During this period, little people were often employed as jesters.

Indoor pastimes

Noblemen and women played such board games as chess and backgammon. Dice games were often played for money. Music, singing, and dancing were popular with rich and poor alike. Folk dances enjoyed by peasants included chain dances and dance games, such as "Ring-a-Ring O' Roses." Nobles developed more elegant versions of these village dances. For example, they performed the carol, a circle dance, in a slower and grander manner than the lively style of the peasants.

Professional dancers, jugglers, acrobats, and animal trainers wandered from town to town, performing in the town square or on the village green. Dancing was also a popular part of the religious plays performed by the guilds.

A 1300's ivory mirror case shows a knight and lady playing chess. Chess, played in Europe from the 1100's, was popular among nobles.

Nobles perform a round dance in a town square. Peasants entertained themselves with such dance games as "Ring-a-Ring O' Roses."

Troubadours and minstrels

Musicians in the Middle Ages developed several styles of vocal music to use in churches. In the 1100's and 1200's, French poet-composers called troubadours made up songs and poems to perform at the courts of French nobles. In Germany, similar performers were called minnesingers *(MIHN uh SIHNG uhrs).* Their songs often told of a knight's hopeless love for a lady of high social position.

Such professional entertainers were also known as minstrels. A minstrel might be a musician, singer, storyteller, juggler, tumbler (acrobat), or clown. Storytellers also traveled around the countryside, gathering news and passing on stories from one region to another. There were no newspapers in those days, so a traveling entertainer had much to tell as he rested at the local inn and chatted to the villagers. A troubadour knew all the latest gossip and scandals at court. He was expected to compose verses at a moment's notice and to play at least two musical instruments.

Jesters

At court, a king often had a jester, or person whose job was to tell jokes, act the fool, and generally amuse his master. The jester wore a cap with bells. At court banquets, he would sometimes make fun of guests, who had to laugh in spite of their own discomfort—or risk angering the king.

An illustration from an illuminated manuscript from the 1600's shows an orchestra and choir performing from a musicians balcony. Only men and boys played instruments or sang in choirs.

Did You Know?

At the marriage of Princess Margaret of England in 1290, it is said that 426 minstrels were hired to entertain the guests. King Edward I's many court minstrels included two women, who performed under the names of Matill Makejoye and Pearl in the Egg.

Most people in the Middle Ages wore simple clothing made of cloth, animal fur, and leather. They made their own clothes at home, using wool from sheep and linen from flax plants. They spun thread on spinning wheels and wove it into fabric on looms. Wealthy people paid tailors to make clothes that were often costly and fancy.

Builders in the 1400's wear the working clothes of the time: a simple tunic and breeches.

A knight's clothes

Beneath his armor, a knight wore long stockings and a tunic that reached to his knees. This shirtlike garment had sleeves and was made of linen or wool. Over this tunic, the knight wore a sleeveless tunic open at the sides and fastened with a belt. His cloak fastened at the shoulders.

More elegant wear

Women of the early Middle Ages wore simple, loose tunics. Later, they wore long dresses that were laced to fit the upper part of the body. Men wore loose breeches—pants that reached to just below the knee—under their tunics. Some men wore long, brightly colored stockings. Others wrapped long strips of cloth around their legs.

The growing towns in the late Middle Ages had shops run by weavers, tailors, shoemakers, and other craftworkers. They cut, fit, and decorated clothes and shoes with more skill for wealthy customers.

Changes in fashion

During the 1100's and 1200's, women wore metal hairnets, veils, and draped throat covers called wimples. Men wore hoods that had long tails. Both men and women wore outer tunics or long sleeveless garments called surcoats.

By the 1300's, the fashion had changed. Men's surcoats were now hip-length and buttoned down the front. A rich man's clothes might have dozens of buttons, and his jacket was fastened with a belt studded with jewels. On his head, he wore a felt hat decorated with jewels.

In the 1400's, the surcoat was pleated, edged with fur, and fastened at the waist by a belt. The shoulders were padded and the chest stiffened to make the wearer's waist appear smaller. By now, men's shoes had become so pointed that the front was often curled up and fastened to the knee with a small chain.

What Were Hairstyles Like?

- Most men wore their hair shoulder-length.
- Priests and monks had a shaved patch called a tonsure on the crown of their head.
- Girls and unmarried women wore their hair loose. Married women covered their hair with a veil or a hoodlike covering.
- Some women plucked or shaved their hair at the front to make their forehead seem higher—a sign of beauty.

An Italian painting from the 1400's shows nobles at a wedding. The women wear long trailing gowns and tall headdresses. The men wear short tunics, capes, brightly colored stockings, and fancy hats.

The wimple was a throat cover worn by women in Europe during the 1200's, usually with various hoodlike head coverings.

People in the Middle Ages did not shop as often as we do now. They probably went to the market once a month. Some big markets were held once a year. These trade fairs helped encourage the growth of busy cities.

Markets

Farmers went to the market to buy and sell animals, animal products such as wool, and grains when they had more than enough to feed themselves and their livestock. Other people might buy clay pots, a new knife, or a length of rope. People enjoyed going to the market to meet old friends, gossip, and hear news of the world beyond the village.

Banks

As trade grew, so did the need for a better money system. Merchants had been accustomed to carrying gold around with them to pay for what they bought. But gold was heavy to carry and easy to steal. It was safer to have a bank handle your money. Banks were established to save merchants from carrying heavy sacks of gold with them on their business trips.

An illustration from an illuminated manuscript shows a trade fair in a French town in the 1400's. A shepherd drives his flock of sheep into town to be sold as a bishop blesses the fair. Out-of-town merchants display their wares in tents. Local merchants advertise their specialities with signs mounted over their shop doors.

A wooden chest was a useful item of furniture. People kept their valuables in chests that were fastened with heavy metal locks. A trader might keep his gold in a wooden chest or hide it under the floorboards.

Trade fairs

The most popular markets grew into trade fairs. These fairs were held each year in certain cities, and merchants from all over Europe and beyond came to buy and sell goods. They also exchanged ideas with other merchants about new products and production methods. Trade between different parts of Europe grew during the Middle Ages, helping to spread wealth and knowledge.

Trading towns and ports grew into larger cities. Merchants in Flanders (now part of Belgium) flourished, and Flanders became one of the busiest marketplaces in Europe. It was an important center for the wool trade with England across the North Sea, and with other European countries.

Did You Know?

Modern banking began between the 1200's and 1600's in Italy. The word *bank* comes from the Italian word *banco* or *banca*, meaning "bench." Early Italian bankers did business on benches in the street.

An Italian banker in the 1400's conducts business from a bench—*banco* in Italian—on the street.

Going to Sea

Merchants and traders, as well as explorers, went to sea in wooden sailing ships. Most sailors stayed close to shore, but some made daring voyages in search of new lands.

Viking long ships

Among the bravest sailors of the Middle Ages were the Vikings. They came from the lands of Scandinavia that are now Denmark, Norway, and Sweden. The Vikings built long wooden ships powered by oars and a single sail. Some of these ships had as many as 30 oars on each side. A Viking ship sailed well in rough seas or calm waters and was light enough to enter shallow rivers. Trading ships carried goods, families, and farm animals to new lands. Warships, called long ships, carried bands of warriors who set out to raid and plunder.

Viking ships were the best ships in northern Europe between the A.D. 700's and the late 1000's. Bold Vikings sailed their ships across the Atlantic Ocean to Iceland, Greenland, and North America.

The Vikings sailed from Scandinavia in three main directions from the A.D. 700's to the 1000's. The Danes went south and raided Germany, France, England, Spain, and the Mediterranean coast. The Norwegians traveled to North America. The Swedes went to eastern Europe.

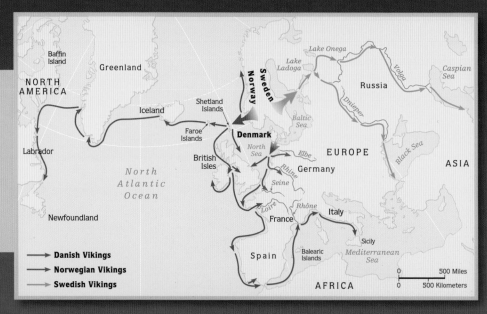

Baffin Island
Greenland
NORTH AMERICA
Iceland
Shetland Islands
Lake Onega
Lake Ladoga
Sweden
Norway
Volga
Caspian Sea
Russia
Faroe Islands
Denmark
Baltic Sea
Dnieper
Labrador
North Sea
British Isles
Elbe
EUROPE
Black Sea
ASIA
North Atlantic Ocean
Germany
Rhine
Seine
Newfoundland
Loire
Rhône
Italy
France
Sicily
Mediterranean Sea
Spain
Balearic Islands
AFRICA

→ Danish Vikings
→ Norwegian Vikings
→ Swedish Vikings

0   500 Miles
0   500 Kilometers

Galleys

On the Mediterranean Sea, people sailed in oared ships called galleys. Galleys had been used in the Mediterranean for hundreds of years, as cargo and passenger ships as well as warships. They had two or even three masts—long poles that supported the sails along with the ropes, chains, and cables. They also had triangular sails called lateens that worked better than square sails when the ship was sailing into the wind. Galleys had oars for use when there was no wind and when the ship was entering or leaving port.

Ships for trade and war

As trade by sea increased, merchants needed roomier ships to carry more goods. By about 1200, shipbuilders in northern Europe had developed a new and sturdy ship called the cog. A cog was wider and deeper than a Viking long ship. It could carry such goods as wool or wine, or it could carry soldiers. The cog had two raised wooden structures called castles— one at the bow (front), and one at the stern (back). The forecastle at the front was a platform from which soldiers could fire arrows and stones at enemy ships. The sterncastle was a shelter for important passengers. Ordinary sailors lived, ate, and slept on deck.

How Did Sailors Find Their Way?

Sailors took sightings of the sun and stars to find out where they were at sea. They also relied on such landmarks as cliffs or islands. By the 1100's, sailors were using magnetic compasses. The first compasses were pieces of magnetic iron floated on straw or cork in a bowl of water. The iron turned to point north. By the 1300's, compasses had a card marked off into 32 points of direction.

The cog was the standard merchant ship and warship in northern Europe from about 1200 to the mid-1400's. Like the Viking ship, it had one large sail.

Famous People

The lives of four very different people show what brought lasting fame in the age of knights and castles.

Charlemagne

Charlemagne *(SHAHR luh MAYN)*, or Charles the Great, ruled the most powerful Christian kingdom of western Europe in the early Middle Ages. He was king of the Franks—people of Europe living in what is now France and Germany. Charlemagne also conquered most of western Europe, including what are now Belgium, Luxembourg, and the Netherlands, as well as most of Italy. On Christmas Day, 800, Charlemagne was crowned emperor of the Romans. His empire laid the foundation for western European politics and culture during the Middle Ages.

Charlemagne was a wise ruler. At his palace, he set up a school for priests and scholars from all over his empire. This school trained teachers for other places of learning throughout Europe. Scholars at the schools collected and copied ancient Roman writings, which otherwise would have been lost.

A painting by the Italian artist Giotto (c. 1266-1337) shows Saint Francis of Assisi preaching to the birds. He was known for his deep respect for nature and love of animals.

Charlemagne was the most famous ruler of the Middle Ages.

Saint Francis of Assisi

Saint Francis of Assisi *(uh SEE zee)* was one of the most popular saints of the Middle Ages. He was born Giovanni Bernardone in about 1181 in Assisi, a small town in Italy. In 1205, he believed he heard a call from God to repair a ruined church near Assisi. He turned away from his wealthy family and friends to live in poverty, preaching and healing the sick. Soon he attracted followers and founded the Franciscan order of friars, or traveling preachers. He died in 1226 and was made a saint two years later. Images of Saint Francis almost always include birds because of his love of animals.

Marco Polo

Marco Polo was the most famous European traveler of the Middle Ages. He was born in Venice, Italy, in 1254. His father and uncle were merchants, and in 1271 they set out on a journey to China. Marco Polo, age 17, went with them.

In China, they were welcomed by Emperor Kublai Khan, who sent Marco on many official tours around his huge empire. No European had seen so much of China before. The Polos began to think they would never return home. Finally they were allowed to escort a Chinese princess to her wedding in Persia. Then they made their way over land to Turkey, and from there to Venice.

The Polos arrived home in 1295, having been away for 24 years. Marco Polo dictated a book about his adventures. He told of the many marvels he had seen, such as how the Chinese used paper money, which was unknown in Europe.

Joan of Arc was a French national heroine.

Marco Polo became famous for his journeys in central Asia and China.

Joan of Arc

Joan of Arc was a simple peasant girl who became the heroine of France. She was born about 1412, at a time when France was being defeated by England during the Hundred Years' War.

Like most peasants, Joan never learned to read or write, but she was deeply religious. At the age of 13 she began hearing what she believed were the voices of saints. These voices persuaded her that God had chosen her to help King Charles VII of France drive the English from French soil. She convinced the king to let her lead his soldiers and inspired the French to victory in several battles. Then, in 1430, she was captured by enemies, who handed her over to the English. The English imprisoned her and accused her of being a witch. Joan insisted her visions and voices came from God, but she was burned at the stake in 1431. She was declared a saint by the Roman Catholic Church in 1920.

Castles were built to last forever. But by the 1300's, the use of gunpowder in warfare meant that new styles of castles were needed. The gun, not the knight, now ruled the battlefield.

Castles with ring walls

Crusader knights who went from Europe to the Middle East brought back new ideas about castle-building. In the East, they had seen castles with rings of walls at different levels. Inside the main wall were a second and a third wall. Huge new castles of this type, called concentric castles, were built from about 1270 in Britain. Most of the large castles built in Wales by King Edward I were concentric. The king hired an expert castle-builder, Master James of St. George, to plan his new castles. They were the finest fortresses of their time.

Gunpowder

Gunpowder was first used in western Europe at the Battle of Crécy, in France, in 1346. This marked the start of a new age in warfare. Gunpowder could explode with enough power to shatter the walls of the strongest castle. Castles built after the mid-1300's reflect the change in fighting methods that followed the first use of this powerful new weapon.

Deal Castle, in Kent, England, was built for King Henry VIII. It took only two years to build (1539-1540), much less time than earlier castles. This castle has six short towers surrounding the central keep. Cannons mounted on the flat tops of the towers could fire at ships.

Bunratty *(bun RAT ee)* Castle in County Clare, Ireland, has a massive box-shaped keep. It dates from the 1400's, when lords built castles as fortified homes.

Castles as homes

By the 1400's, some castles were made of brick, not stone. They were strong and well defended. Some had openings in the walls through which cannon could be fired, but by this time, castles were used as homes, not fortresses. The castle owner did not expect to fight off a siege or keep a company of armed knights.

But people continued to build castles. In the 1500's, Henry VIII of England had a series of new castles built to defend the southeast coast of England. These castles had guns that could fire at ships, and they had short towers called bastions instead of tall towers.

The end of armor

By the 1500's, people wore armor mainly to take part in tournaments and ceremonial occasions. The Spanish soldiers who conquered the Aztecs of Mexico wore chest armor. But by the 1600's, few soldiers wore armor on the battlefield. It was too heavy and could not protect soldiers against handguns and cannon.

◄ Beaumaris *(bewe MAR is)* Castle in north Wales was built for King Edward I of England in the late 1200's to early 1300's. It is a good example of the concentric or ring castle that was especially difficult to capture. This type of castle owed much to the influence of crusaders, who had seen such castles in the East.

Castles Around the World

Many castles were built in Europe during the Middle Ages, but people in other parts of the world also built castles.

The Moors built castles in North Africa and in the parts of Spain that they ruled. Portuguese traders who sailed to Africa built trading forts similar to castles along the African coast. People in Korea, Japan, and India also built castles.

Make way for the elephants

Indian castles were much like those of Europe and the Middle East, though often more richly decorated. The gate of an Indian castle was also higher—high enough for an elephant to walk through!

In India, elephants were used in battles. Soldiers rode on elephants' backs inside small wooden shelters that looked like miniature castles. An elephant could break down the wooden doors of a castle just by pushing against them with its head. To prevent this, castle doors usually had long iron spikes sticking out from the wood.

North African castles have changed little over the centuries. Taourirt Kasbah, a castle in Morocco, looks ancient but was built in the 1930's in the style of earlier North African castles.

Jaisalmer Fort in Rajasthan, India, was built in 1156. Like castles in Europe, it has stone walls with towers. Local rulers in India built castles as symbols of their power.

Castles of Japan

The Japanese began to build stone castles in the late 1500's. These castles were tall buildings surrounded by water-filled moats. The castle stood on a stone base, but the upper walls were made of wood and plaster and were not strong enough to stand up to artillery (heavy guns). This did not matter greatly. When these castles were built, there were few cannon in Japan. Most battles were fought on open ground between armies of samurai warriors.

The samurai were knights. They wore armor, and their main weapons were curved swords and bows and arrows. They were proud of their ancient traditions and were bound by a code of loyalty to their lords, who were called daimyos. The samurai were graded in military ranks, each rank being paid an appropriate amount in rice.

Fortress of the Inca

About 1520, the Inca built a massive fortress beside their royal city of Cusco in Peru. It was called Sacsayhuaman. Some of its stones weigh 100 tons (91 metric tons). The builders set these huge stones together without using mortar. They cut and shaped each stone to fit against the others, like pieces of a giant jigsaw puzzle. When Spanish soldiers conquered Cusco, they used stones from the fortress to build houses.

Osaka Castle stands on a hill in the city of Osaka, Japan. It was completed in the 1580's and rebuilt in the early 1600's after suffering damage in a war.

Castles Today

People enjoy visiting castles. In some castles, we may admire works of art, suits of armor, and old weapons. In others, we can peer into dark, grim dungeons or prison cells. Castles are now among the top tourist attractions in the world.

The Alhambra in Granada, Spain, was built by the Moors between 1248 and 1354 and contains many fine examples of Moorish art.

Pretend castles

From the 1700's, architects in Europe began copying the styles of the Middle Ages to build mock-castles. These looked like old castles, but they were not meant for warfare. Wealthy people chose to live in mansions that looked like Scottish fortresses or French castles. Some people even had castle ruins built in the parks of their country houses.

Modern knights

Knights no longer fight on the battlefield. But enthusiasts still dress up in armor and demonstrate knights' skills to entertain crowds. Castles that are open to the public stage displays of jousting on horseback and archers shooting with bows and arrows. Guests may enjoy a medieval-style banquet in the castle hall.

Neuschwanstein (*noy SHVAHN shtyn*) Castle in Bavaria, Germany, is a romantic version of a castle that knights might have lived in. The castle was built between 1869 and 1886 for King Ludwig II of Bavaria, who was known as Mad King Ludwig.

Today, mock-battles are performed for entertainment. Visitors watch knights joust and other displays that bring the Middle Ages to life.

Castle Facts

- The biggest castle is Prague Castle in the Czech Republic. You could fit 13 football fields inside its walls!

- The widest moats surround the Imperial Palace in Beijing, China. They are 150 feet (46 meters) wide.

- The biggest castle still used as a residence is Windsor Castle in England. It is used as a home by Queen Elizabeth II.

Windsor Castle, which is near London, is one of the official residences of the British monarchy. In addition to the keep, 14 towers rise from the walls surrounding the castle. It is the largest occupied castle in the world and the longest continually occupied castle in the world—more than 800 years.

A castle near Tours, France—Chateau de Chenonceau—spans a river in the Loire Valley. Chenonceau was built in the 1500's as a luxurious country house for a noble family. The Loire Valley is known for its chateaux—or castles—which are considered among the most beautiful in the world.

cannon a powerful, tube-shaped gun that is too large to be carried by hand.

cathedral a large or important church.

empire a group of nations or states under one ruler or government, with one country having some measure of control over the rest.

fort a strong building or place that can be defended against an enemy; fortified place.

fortress a large fort built with walls and defenses.

guild a union of people in the same trade or craft in the Middle Ages.

Hundred Years' War a series of wars between England and France from 1337 to 1453.

joust a combat between two knights on horseback, armed with lances, especially as part of a tournament.

lance a long wooden spear with a sharp iron or steel head.

manor a large estate controlled by a lord in the Middle Ages. Peasants lived on part of this land in return for goods, services, or rent.

minstrel a professional entertainer who played and sang and recited poems.

moat a deep, wide trench often filled with water, dug around a castle or town to keep enemies out.

monastery a house or group of buildings in which monks live, work, and pray together.

monk a man who belongs to a religious order and lives in a monastery.

Moors people from North Africa, who conquered and lived in parts of Spain from 711 to 1492.

Muslim a follower of Muhammad; believer in Islam, the religion founded by him.

Normans a group of Vikings who first settled in northern France, then advanced into England, southern Italy, and Sicily. Norman warriors began their conquests in the 800's.

Parliament; parliament the national lawmaking body of Great Britain and Northern Ireland that developed from a council of nobles and high-ranking clergy that advised the early kings of England; a council or congress that is the highest lawmaking body in some countries.

peasant someone who works on a small farm, or the owner of a small farm.

pilgrim a person who travels to an important holy place, such as a shrine, for a religious purpose.

Roman; Roman Empire of or having to do with ancient Rome or its people; the empire of ancient Rome that controlled most of Europe and the Middle East from 27 B.C. to A.D. 476.

tapestry a decorated woven cloth used for wall coverings, furniture, or windows.

tournament a series of military exercises in which knights fought to show off their skill and courage.

troubadour a poet who wrote love songs. Troubadours were popular in Europe from the 1000's to the 1200's.

vassal a person who held land from a superior and swore loyalty in return.

Books

The Age of Feudalism by Timothy L. Biel (Lucent Books, 1994)

Castle by Stephen Biesty and Richard Platt (Dorling Kindersley, 1994)

The Kingfisher Atlas of the Medieval World by Simon Adams and Kevin W. Maddison (Kingfisher, 2007)

Knight by Geoff Dann (A.A. Knopf, 1993)

Knights and Castles: 50 Hands-On Activities to Experience the Middle Ages by Avery Hart and Paul Mantell (Williamson Publishers, 1998)

Life in the Middle Ages: The Castle by Kathryn Hinds (Benchmark Books, 2001)

A Medieval Cathedral by Fiona Macdonald and John James (Peter Bedrick Books, 1991)

Medieval Warfare by Tara Steele (Crabtree Publishing Co., 2004)

The Middle Ages by Mike Corbishley (Chelsea House, 2007)

Richard the Lionheart: The Life of a King and Crusader by David West and Jackie Gaff (Rosen Publishing Group, 2005)

Websites

Britain's Bayeux Tapestry
www.bayeuxtapestry.org.uk

A replica of the famous Bayeux Tapestry can be seen section-by-section at this site, provided by the Reading Museum Service. You can also read more about the people and events that appear throughout the tapestry.

British History In-Depth: The Middle Ages
http://www.bbc.co.uk/history/british/middle_ages/

Tour the medieval churches of Britain, follow the reigns of King John and Richard I, and test your medieval battlefield wits in the Battlefield Academy game on this site from the BBC.

Castles on the Web
http://www.castlesontheweb.com

Browse a database full of information on castles, palaces, abbeys, and churches.

Interactives: Middle Ages
www.learner.org/interactives/middleages/

This website provides an interactive look at the medieval world, with trivia questions whose answers include links to more information.

The Labyrinth: Resources for Medieval Studies
http://labyrinth.georgetown.edu

This website, sponsored by Georgetown University, provides links to a wide variety of materials about the medieval world.

The Middle Ages
www.mnsu.edu/emuseum/history/middleages

Choose your guide—a knight, a merchant, a nun, or a peasant—through the realms of the medieval Europe. Your guide will lead you to information about government, trade, literature, village life, and many other topics.

The Middle Ages.net
www.themiddleages.net

This website contains a directory of famous medieval people, links on weaponry and warfare, and a special section on the dreaded Black Death.

Secrets of Lost Empires: Medieval Siege
http://www.pbs.org/wgbh/nova/lostempires/trebuchet/

Follow NOVA's team of experts as they recreate a medieval trebuchet. Slide shows illustrate the weaponry and warfare of the Middle Ages.